michelle kabele

JUST SAY

The Power of Creative Thinking Way Outside the Tired, Old Box

ISBN: 9780982068632

Table of Contents

INTRODUCTION: You're Not the Crazy One

"Oh, please…" you think with sarcasm, as you hear it again. If someone tells you one more time to "think outside the box," or "think outside the box but be in the box," you're going to scream, right? I mean, how many times have you heard that phrase when it comes to growing your business? Well, don't worry. I won't feed you that tired cliché again. In fact, in this book, I'm going to ask you to just drop-kick that box! That's right! Boot it out of your life!

You see, the problem with that thinking is that it still refers to a box, to something with limited space…and thus limited possibilities. So even if you are truly thinking outside of it, you're still wasting time and energy trying to circumvent it. And if it's still in the picture, you can bet that certain parts of your business—and your thinking—are being relegated to it, whether you realize it or not. Just get rid of the darn thing here and now.

While you're at it, disconnect from anyone in your circle who is still preoccupied with the box. Whether they're stuck in it or just running around the perimeter, they're locked into counterproductive thinking that's probably holding **you** back, too. They're hemmed in by their own limitations. They're intimidated by ideas that threaten to take them outside their comfort zones. They are the vanilla—the *Naysayers*.

Unbridled by the restrictive bonds of negative expectations, you can take your business into uncharted territory. It's the way of the men and women who have brought us things like the telephone, once called an "electric toy" by the Naysayers. In the realm of business, your distinctions propel you farther than your competition in the marketplace.

In the words of Walter Lippman, "When all think alike, no one is thinking."

So, forego the Naysayers and think for yourself!

CHAPTER 1: And They Said It Couldn't Be Done

> "Once we rid ourselves of traditional thinking, we can get on with creating the future."
> **JAMES BERTRAND**

Long gone are the days when business and creativity were considered mutually exclusive terms. Oh, there are still stubborn pessimists who staunchly decry the glory of non-linear, forward thinking solutions…but they live in that box, remember? So don't worry about them! Yes, creative thinking is the privilege of more than just artists and wandering gypsies. In fact, it might do you well to start thinking of creativity as more than just a frivolous leisure pursuit, but as an integral part of a successful business. Consider some of the top business, marketing, and entrepreneurial geniuses of all time, and you might just change your thinking.

• • • • • •

There is no more unlikely billionaire in the history of the world than **Richard Branson**. Learning disorders were not handled with today's proactive compassion in the U.K. school system (private or public) during the 1950s and 1960s, when Branson struggled with dyslexia. With virtually no academic success to his credit, he was branded a failure early on. By the ripe old age of 15, though, he had already started two businesses: growing Christmas trees and raising parakeets. Although both ventures eventually failed, he ignored the "I told you so's" of the naysaying masses and followed his entrepreneurial spirit.

What would become Virgin Records and the Virgin Megastore chain began with a high school dropout selling cutouts and discounted records from the trunk of his car. Now, roughly 40 years later, Branson has amassed a mind-boggling list of successful businesses to his credit. From Virgin Mobile to Virgin Atlantic Airways to Virgin Health Bank (a center where parents can store their baby's umbilical cord blood stem cells in private and public stem cell banks after the birth), there is no market that this businessman's creative enthusiasm won't tackle. Why, there's even Virgin Galactic; founded in 2004, it just could be the tourism company that books your first trip into suborbital space. Naysayers, be damned!

Perhaps most impressive is what great, unfettered, fearless minds can do for humanity. The Virgin Earth Challenge will award $25 million to the individual or group who can create a commercially viable design that can remove greenhouse gases each year for at least 10 years without harmful effects and stabilize the earth's environment. Pretty impressive achievements for a man who was once told he'd never amount to anything!

• • • • • •

Tom Peters is another shining example of rising above the negative thinkers. He took on not only his own personal visions, but also set out to change the way we manage business on a national level. And he succeeded! While Peter Drucker made management a subject worthy of study, Peters began elevating that study to the next level in the 1970s. In leading us away from a proscriptive, from-the-top-down management style, he ushered in a whole new corporate environment. Peters has been called the "uber-guru" of management and the "father of the post-modern corporation." It's been an uphill battle all along. We see corporations stuck in archaic management systems all the time. In fact, you've probably worked for a few of them!

In one triumphant leap, Peters published *In Search of Excellence* in 1982. This book set American businesses on a new course, hurtling forever away from the bottom line to a focus on people, customers, culture, action, and a "perpetual, self-renewing entrepreneurial spirit." You can't turn the tide in corporate America when you're listening to people say, "It's always been done this other way." Peters brought a new mantra of personal value, of empowered decision makers to every level of a corporation. More than 20 years later, he continues to find new angles and insights on that message—ever honing it for our benefit!

• • • • • •

Speaking of the benefit of the masses, let's not overlook Apple Inc., and its innovative, unstoppable, unwavering CEO, **Steve Jobs**. In the late 1970s, long before the advent of the IBM PC, Jobs made the easy and affordable personal computer available to consumers with the help of Apple co-founder Steve Wozniak. While his classmates were attending high school dances and football practice, Jobs (in his own quirky, Silicon Valley, budding entrepreneurial style) frequented lectures at Hewlett Packard. He later enrolled in college, only to drop out after one semester. Oh, but he still audited some important classes…like calligraphy…to which he attributes Mac's multiple typefaces and balance of design and aesthetics. So, there you go. Where would Mac be if young Jobs had enrolled in English 101 like the peers who chided him?

At the age of 20, after a brief stint as a technician at Atari, Jobs set off to backpack through India in search of enlightenment, nurturing what he calls his "countercultural roots" and experimenting with LSD. With no regard for those who would have him stay in "The Valley," immersed in the hub of the computer industry, he must have found something at least akin to enlightenment because he returned from that trip and founded Apple computers. Years later, in 1986, Jobs acquired the computer graphics division of Lucasfilm Ltd., better known as Pixar Animation Studios. He remained CEO and majority shareholder until Walt Disney Company acquired it in 2006. He is still its largest individual shareholder and sits on its Board of Directors.

In a CBS *60 Minutes* interview, Jobs said, "My model for business is The Beatles. They were four guys that kept each other's negative tendencies in check—they balanced each other. And the total was greater than the sum of the parts. Great things in business are not done by one person. They are done by a team of people." Jobs might hold up Eleanor Rigby to the Naysayers and say, "Ah, look at all the lonely people…"

• • • • • •

Of course, let's not forget **Bill Gates**, the super-geek who founded Microsoft with Paul Allen and ended up as the world's third richest person. Not a bad outcome for a Harvard dropout who teamed up with a buddy to work on computer chips. While Gates had the emotional and financial backing of a wealthy family, that environment gave him a whole other set of expectations to rise above. Imagine the flack he took for walking away from the Ivy League education that most would give their right arm for, especially after scoring 1590 out of a possible 1600 on his SATs!

Gates created his first computer program in the eighth grade. Programming in BASIC, his skills were recognized by outside companies. Soon, he and his cohorts were hired to write payroll programs, among others, before they even graduated from high school. When Intel released its 8080 CPU, Gates realized it was the first computer chip priced under $200 that could run BASIC. Voila! A user-friendly and affordable chip, perfect for a personal computer. Having set the stage, he made his entrance with co-star Allen, and Microsoft was born. After they partnered with IBM in 1980, Windows came along and revolutionized our world. Where would we be if Gates and Jobs hadn't followed their creative minds?

• • • • • •

No list of success stories is complete without the mention of **Oprah Winfrey**. Who would have thought that an African American girl born in abject poverty to teenage parents—and later shuffled between each of her single parents and her grandmother—would one day be considered the most influential woman in the world?

Molested and raped as a preadolescent, Oprah gave birth to a son at age 14, but the child soon died. After going to live with her father, though, she excelled in school and earned a full scholarship to Tennessee State University. She went on to be the youngest and the first black news anchor at Nashville's WLAC-TV. The girl who once wore dresses made from potato sacks is now an Academy Award-nominated actress with the highest rated talk show in the history of television and a philanthropy record exceeding $50,000,000, thanks to her Oprah's Angel Network. Amazing what a little determination can accomplish!

• • • • • •

And how about a free-thinking genius who took the Internet from federal defense surveillance to a hub for commerce? You can thank **Jeff Bezos** that brilliant move. A graduate of Princeton and employee of Wall Street, Bezos heard the larger calling of the Internet in 1994. Noticing that its usage was increasing by a whopping 2,300 percent per year, he knew this incredible resource could serve the world in a yet incomprehensible way.

Reviewing the top 20 mail order businesses, Bezos decided that books were the one commodity that would best be served by the Internet because a comprehensive hard-copy catalogue was impossible. All he needed was a single location on the Internet for consumers to access book wholesalers' inventory lists. He wrote out the business plan on a cross-country trip, typing while his wife drove. They would call their business Amazon, after the seemingly endless river and its numerous fingers.

In July of 1995, Bezos started doing business in a makeshift home office. Two months later, his business was bringing in $20,000 a week. Amazon.com went public in 1997. Naturally, skeptics doubted he could keep pace when traditional corporate booksellers started selling their wares on the Internet. Two years later, Amazon had a greater market share than its competitors combined and Borders, the bookselling superstore, was looking to strike a deal for its Internet traffic. Still, Bezos had bigger and better things in mind, aiming to bring consumers everything under the sun—not just books. Again, the cynics shook their heads at his folly, confident that Bezos could never keep pace with it all. He proved them wrong time and time again. When the dot-com boom imploded, Amazon kept restructuring, focusing on its core values: customer obsession, ownership, bias for action, frugality, high hiring bar, and innovation. While the Naysayers drown in the muddy waters of mediocrity, people like Bezos are floating on a crystal clear river of abundance. Long flow the Amazon!

QUOTE THE NAYSAYER

"The horse is here today, but the automobile is only a novelty—a fad."

President of Michigan Savings Bank, advising against investing in the Ford Motor Company

CHAPTER 2: The Curse of the Negative Thinker

> "When you wholeheartedly adopt a 'with all your heart' attitude and go out with the positive principle, you can do incredible things."
>
> **Norman Vincent Peale**

Negative thinking is detrimental to any organization. That's a given, right? Yet that productivity-draining virus lurks in conference rooms, at water coolers, and through emails that pass from one employee to another. It's easy to smugly serve up sour criticism but much more difficult to seek alternative answers. Keep that in mind when someone maliciously derails the brilliant distribution plan you've spent a week refining. You'll usually find that this naysayer offers no constructive criticism or creative solutions.

This type of overt negativity may ruffle your feathers a bit, which is the naysayer's diversion tactic used to distract you from the truth that this person has nothing of value to contribute. If intended to be helpful, the opinion would be accompanied by a thoughtful suggestion, advice, or feasible alternative. A good deal of negative thinking comes cleverly disguised (or sometimes merely thinly veiled) as well-meaning advice or redirection.

So, how do you deal with the seeds of negativity in your business? Well, you can turn and walk away from it. Shrug it off. Ignore the bad karma. But, like a bandage over a cut, it merely masks the injury rather than treats it. Instead, let's look at how to confront the naysayer's block.

A CRUSHING CONTAGION

We've all experienced comments and conversations which, on the surface, seem to be saying one thing but leave you wondering if you are just reading between the lines—or creating a whole fictional subtext. There you stand, wasting time and energy, trying to figure out what just transpired. You wonder about the other person or people and perhaps second-guess yourself.

That's the insidious nature of negative thinking. When it is expressed—covertly or blatantly—it cultivates more negative thinking. Bursting the bubble of positive thinking is like someone with a nasty cold sneezing into a crowd without covering his or her mouth. The contagious virus is projected out there where it will spread like wildfire, leveling the healthy ones in its path. Some people have a natural resistance to the virus, others consciously fight it off, but many succumb to the germ of doubt and criticism. People start to feel badly. Productivity and morale suffer attrition. The virus morphs, adapting itself to weakened immunities caused by the initial virus and spreading to those who were once resistant. The thing is, no one remembers the initial contamination. Everyone just walks around feeling crappy, spreading questions and blame about all of the illness floating around.

It's the same with negative thinking in your organization. One person sets in motion a negative belief system or opinion.

"That won't work."

"We can't change the way we've been doing things."

"Why risk failure?"

Even those who don't buy into the naysaying initially are subject to the viral spread of its message as it, too, morphs and changes. Even if your team members aren't completely "stricken," they will be affected in one way or another, even if it's just by working with deflated, uninspired, and doubtful colleagues.

Let's look at an example of how this downward spiral can affect your workplace. First, recognize that 70–80 percent of your business comes from existing customers. Go ahead. Look at your sales figures. Now, let's say you are ready to implement a new marketing plan that will open up a new niche for your business. Assuming that you are not one of the negative thinkers, let's inject one detractor into the discussion of the launch. The naysayer casts doubt on the sales potential of the new market segment you plan to explore. Ah, fear of the unknown is a common trigger for the naysayer. So what happens next? Even if you don't pull the plan or revise it, you—or members of your team may doubt its viability or, worse yet, your intentions for it.

Even if this negative thinking is couched in terms that make it seem altruistic, it makes you stumble and twitter away valuable time in a circular conversation with yourself as you weigh the viability of your own knowledge with the theory of your dissenters. Faster than you can say, "How did that happen?" a major percentage of your clients and customers are affected by the trickle down, viral effect of negative thinking in your organization.

Even if your marketing plan is flawed, know that you are building it upon a solid foundation of your experience, not a flimsy whim. If there were no room for error, there would be no room for growth or improvement! How many trials do you think Thomas Edison endured before the light bulb—or any one of the brilliant inventions that he contributed to our world—paid off for him?

Edison said, "I am not discouraged, because every wrong attempt discarded is another step forward." If that belief is good enough for the "Father of Invention," it should be good enough for you, personally and professionally.

The next time you encounter negative thinking, stop and consider its crippling potential. Then, stop and consider the viral effect of perseverance and positive thinking! If Edison had allowed his creative, ambitious thinking to be diminished by people who called him crazy, the results of his greatest invention would have been delayed. Oh sure, someone would eventually have shed light on our world, but when?

So don't deprive the world of the benefits of your creative potential. And don't let it hamper the forward-thinking momentum of your team. Many people are waiting with open minds, ready to embrace what you have to offer. Bring it on! And give it to them with the unwavering faith that, as their needs evolve, so do your skills and resources. In fact, what you bring them probably drives their evolving needs, and there's a lot of potential for growth.

QUOTE THE NAYSAYER

"Everything that can be invented has been invented."

Charles H. Duell, Director of U.S. Patent Office, 1899

CHAPTER 3: Creating Creativity

M. A. ROSANOFF:

"Mr. Edison, please tell me what laboratory rules you want me to observe."

THOMAS EDISON:

"There ain't no rules around here. We're trying to accomplish somep'n!"

We've all heard the nature versus nurture concepts as they apply to human development. Well, guess what? The influences of our inner being and what happens in the world around us reverberate far beyond the early years. In fact, your workplace environment is a direct result of the quantity and the quality of the productivity in your organization — and vice versa. And, that productivity hinges upon the level of creativity that is allowed and fostered in the workplace.

Twenty or thirty years ago, no one questioned the viability of hundreds of people in one office working independently in isolated, small cubicles. Walls, of any kind, were a good thing, creating separation. Well, times they are a changin'! Thanks to a growing number of forward-thinking professionals, the modern workplace has become a canvas for the evolution of human potential. People are coming to realize that "environment" implies more than a physical setting. A positive environment is also a mindset, an intention on building a corporate culture that is fueled by another 21st century term: ideation (the positive flow of creative thinking!).

For your team members to infuse their work with this power of creative thinking, they must be free to operate in an environment where they are, at the very least, open to each other's suggestions and ideas (and preferably welcome such input). They must feel free to challenge the status quo and explore new ideas. Embrace the ideators because they will deliver your success!

This type of positive, creative environment then fuels a dynamic culture where people throughout the organization can actively engage in developing new ideas and improve processes at work—even if it is by trial and error. From a management perspective, creating this atmosphere is less about inding a few outstanding creative individuals to save the company. It is more about establishing the conditions that draw out the creative potential of everyone on your team. By extension, this dynamic energy will translate to the rest of your organization. Positive energy can be just as viral as the negative. It's your choice which one to foster.

In a nutshell, creativity thrives when people freely share their *knowledge* and *opinions*—which are not to be confused with information. Information is important, too, but it is static data. Knowledge is a sumptuous blend of experience and wisdom that circulates when people are engaged in dynamic exchanges with one another. These exchanges then take on their own viral qualities. But, unlike the bitter bite of the Naysayer, this type of virus is a healing one. When your team members share their knowledge, it will grow. As the knowledge base broadens, it will give life to new ideas that will keep your entire team energized. Feed the individual, and the individual will feed the group!

STIR THE CREATIVE JUICES.

So, how do you protect and encourage your team's creativity? When you accomplish the following, your team will be in the prime spot for the ultimate in creative thinking!

- Provide spaces that foster a horizontal community, rather than a from-the-top-down design. Creativity is not a measure of a person's status within the company.
- Schedule a regular brainstorming session with your team, focusing on finding solutions to a specific challenge. Set it up in a casual atmosphere, and be sure to serve refreshments! The creative mind thrives when it is fed.
- Create spaces for both formal and informal interactions. Establish a comfortable sitting area where people can put their feet up and not be separated by desks. Model it after your favorite coffee house and bring in a great coffee bar. A little caffeine doesn't hurt….

- Set up an idea board where people can post thoughts, questions, photos, articles, and other bits of inspiration.
- Reward creative effort! From offering a simple "thank you" to a gift or prize, reinforce the value of creative thinking by acknowledging and rewarding the members who take the time to think and present ideas. Such recognition builds confidence and will likely inspire others to join in.

Your team needs a wide range of work settings (perhaps wider than you are accustomed to). Even if you don't have the capacity to physically alter the environment, you can encourage and facilitate group meetings and exchanges and allow individuals more latitude. You never know where the next great meeting-of-minds will occur and who will be the creative catalyst that will take your company to a higher level. There are no benchwarmers on your team. Let everyone play. Those benchwarmers can wait outside your stadium!

A creative team is the product of a creative leader. If you are still working in a metaphoric cubicle in your mind, dismantle it quickly, and start mingling with your team. Spark each other's thinking, and you'll set off a chain reaction of brilliant creative initiatives!

QUOTE THE NAYSAYER

"Sensible and responsible women do not want to vote."

President Grover Cleveland, 1905

CHAPTER 4: Where Do Great Ideas Come From?

> "Disneyland will never be completed. It will continue to grow as long as there is imagination left in the world."
>
> **WALT DISNEY**

Survival in any realm, let alone growth and prosperity, has always hinged upon the ability to adapt and change—and change always begins with the idea of change. The concept precipitates the action. That's also the distinction between the naysayers and the "movers and shakers." Naysayers get stuck on the mere idea of change. YOU, on the other hand, are jazzed by it! You see the potential, harness your inhibitions, and plow fearlessly onward. Okay, maybe not fearlessly, but you keep moving, knowing that there is power for positive change in your ideas.

Today, information, knowledge, and intellectual property can be transmitted at the speed it takes to hit the "Send" button. Your longevity in the market (not to mention your company's longevity) depends increasingly on your ability to generate a constant stream of new ideas that can be efficiently translated to new products, technology, services, and processes. Keeping up with these demands means thinking way beyond the standard procedures manual sitting on your shelf. In fact, that outdated manual might be most handy if you stand on it to get a better look at what's on the horizon! Get the future in your sights and then imagine yourself, your team, and your company marching triumphantly toward it. To make the journey, you'll need imaginative approaches to communication, risk taking, and group efforts.

It may seem like a daunting task, ushering in all of this creative thinking and these new ideas! It's really quite simple, though, and here's a conundrum to help you. The solution to bringing in great new creative ideas is this: *think creatively about thinking creatively.*

Huh?

What that means is that the great new ideas for which you search are all around you…and all around your team. They are hidden in plain sight. You just have to adjust your vision a bit to see them. The foundation for bringing that future into focus lies in freeing up those ideas. And that happens when you create the kind of environment I described in the previous chapter. With that established, your newest task is to listen to and to facilitate the conversations among your team members.

Ask yourself these questions:

- Where have the great ideas come from within your organization in the past?
- Where can they *potentially* come from?
- Where do they come from in your industry?
- What kind of emerging technologies could benefit you and your clients? Look at the emergence of mobile technology. If you didn't want to jump into manufacturing phones, you could do well just by making the accessories for them! Or create ringtones, games, and services that millions of cell phone users crave!
- Can you put a unique spin on the valued elements that you add to your customers' computer technology?
- What was your last great marketing innovation, and how can you update or piggyback on it to propel you and your team to the next level?

You can bet that Walt Disney asked questions like these over and over again in his lifetime. The legacy he built undoubtedly continues that tradition. And although Walt passed away decades ago, the empire he created grows stronger every year because he established a crystal clear vision. Not bad for a man who placed a big talking mouse at the center of his dream. And you think you have dissenters?

The bottom line is, it doesn't matter whether your industry revolves around fantasy or technology. What matters is that it revolves around—and evolves from—an incessant exchange of ideas. As long as you can share and process knowledge and allow your team to do the same, the constant flow of energy can't help but propel your organization continually forward.

QUOTE THE NAYSAYER

"Who the hell wants to hear actors talk?"

Harry M. Warner, Warner Bros Pictures, 1927

CHAPTER 5: The Idea Report Card

"The way to get good ideas is to get lots of ideas and throw the bad ones away."

DR. LINUS PAULING

Okay, so you've got the ideas flowing in your team. People are feeling energized by your encouragement to bring innovation to the fore. Great! Now, what do you do with all of these ideas?

Ideas are creative expressions, unlike the statistics in a quarterly report (although we know that accountants can certainly get creative!). They are the seed from which your next marketing blitz blooms. The fruits of your success are harvested when you have cultivated these little beauties!

Presenting ideas inherently means presenting something new and different. Nothing is more appetizing to a naysayer than a new idea because it feeds their need to criticize. You can prepare yourself for the inevitable negative onslaught by thinking through your idea—not entirely, but with a good degree of consideration. Too much thought might cause you to dismiss the idea. I mean, how could someone create a vast empire from a talking mouse or make millions on cookies? Imagine if Walt Disney gave up too soon! Don't give in to the inner critic. Give your idea a little air to breathe first.

But how do you separate the gems from the duds? You can start by looking at the possibilities:

- How is my idea different from what's already available? Unless you have a definitive answer to this question, stop right now and go back to the drawing board. If you can't be radically different from another success, don't go there. Copycats—even if they're not exact replicas —are not bound for success.

- What will it take to make this idea a reality? Itemize the steps that will be required, one baby step at a time. For example, detail the changes that you'll have to make in your organization to make room for this next great idea.
- What are the costs in terms of capital, manpower, and timing? If you don't have the resources available to support the development, can you find them somewhere?
- What is the size of the market for this idea? You need to know if the market is large enough to support your idea and sustain it over time. How is your idea scoring so far?

GRADING ON A CURVE

Certainly, you're not the only one in your organization who should be thinking creatively. If that's the case, maybe you're not dishing out enough encouragement!

If you are being presented with new ideas, you should have a system in place for evaluating those thoughts. In addition to the questions already posed, put the following items on the Idea Report Card:

- Are there elements of the proposed plan/idea that are borrowed from previously successful measures? If so, how much of the idea is unique? You'll need to tread carefully on the intellectual property field.
- Gauge the validity of the person presenting the idea. What is the person's track record? Take this one with a grain of salt. Every now and then, even a blind squirrel finds a nut.
- Is the idea well-structured? If so, the follow-through probably will be, too.
- Even if the entire idea isn't feasible as presented, can parts of it be modified or improved upon and executed? Mine the gems of that idea!

Finding the next great idea is like mining for diamonds or diving for oysters and their pearls. It's a messy job and not one that you can do without making yourself vulnerable. But the reward can be invaluable.

The next question is, what kind of risk are you willing to assign to the process of reaping the reward? The bottom line is that it can be downright scary to even attempt to assess the validity of something that is merely conceptual. It is human nature to want to know that when you take a step, you are placing yourself on solid ground.

If venturing into this territory is still intimidating to you, heed the advice from Richard Florida in *America's Looming Creativity Crisis:*

> *"To stay innovative, America must continue to attract the world's sharpest minds. And to do that, it needs to invest in the further development of its creative sector. Because wherever creativity goes—and, by extension, wherever talent goes—innovation and economic growth are sure to follow."*

In other words, the future of business will be largely rooted in creative thinking. Increasingly, the benefits outweigh the risks. So, the naysayers who cannot endorse a risk actually immerse themselves in the worst risk of all: apathy and unwitting failure in the marketplace.

If the risk is calculated and the team is energized around it, take it!

QUOTE THE NAYSAYER

"Heavier than air flying machines are impossible."

Lord Kelvin, President, Royal Society, 1895

CHAPTER 6: This Won't Hurt a Bit

> "The essential part of creativity is not being afraid to fail."
>
> **EDWIN H. LAND**

Change. Depending on your mood, your environment, or maybe even your genetic pre-disposition, the word can either excite you or scare the heck out of you. Prevailing opinion, though, says that when change comes knocking for most people, it brings plenty of baggage full of dread.

Why is that?

1. **Fear of the unknown:** People tend to fear what they don't recognize or understand. After the terrorist attacks of 9/11, people feared every stranger on an airplane and every piece of unidentified mail because we didn't know when and where the next attack would hit. It's hard enough when you're presented with cold, hard facts and expected to change based on them. How much more uncertainty do you feel when you are handed a "great idea" that creates a buzz and gains momentum? If people don't understand the "change" itself, they will undoubtedly fear its outcome.

2. **Uncertain outcome:** People like to make wise investments. Call it ego or call it survival skills, most people don't want to put their time and energy into something that might not pay off.

3. **Accountability:** Like it or not, consciously engaging in change sets up a certain amount of expectations for follow-through and follow-up. Can you hear the groan from the Naysaing crowd? Change sets things and people in motion. Sometimes people are more afraid of their own potential (or lack of it) than they are the change agent itself. Most of the time, they fear that they either won't live up to their own potential or expectations, or they fear that they have the capacity to do so but will have to work harder than they would like to.

4. **Loss of comfort zone:** There's nothing like change to shake people out of their comfortable seats and dismantle the world as they know it. Vulnerability is a scary state for most people. It's also the place with the most potential for growth.

It's not up to you to change human nature. Regardless of how well prepared you are, some people will be intimidated by what it is you bring, your creative ideas, and your invitation to participate in them. Face it. Some people will just never get it! Your responsibility is to make sure that your message is as clear, concise, passionate, researched, and documented as it possibly can be, not to make Believers out of Naysayers.

Bottom line? As the messenger, you can't force people to accept the change you propose, but you can make sure that your message is delivered under optimal conditions. Change brings uncertainty under the best of circumstances. Making it as palatable as possible alleviates some of the tension surrounding it.

So fear not and dive headlong into your own sea of change. If you feel yourself start to flail around, remember the words of General Eric Shinseki, Chief of Staff, U.S. Army. "If you don't like change, you're going to like irrelevance even less."

QUOTE THE NAYSAYER

"What use could the company make of an electric toy?"

Western Union, when it turned down rights to the telephone in 1878

CHAPTER 7: And the Geeks Shall Inherit the World

"I would love to change the world, but they won't give me the source code."

UNKNOWN

Freaks and geeks. No doubt every one of the people profiled in the opening chapter was considered one or the other or both in younger days. A Harvard dropout, a high school student who attended lectures at Hewlett Packard (by choice), a brilliant innovator who credits his business model to The Beatles? What made these people stand out from the crowd *then* is what makes them lead the way now.

What is it? They are exactly the kind of creative thinkers we've been talking about here. The equation is simple: passion, debunking of the status quo, and an unwavering belief that they can create something better than what exists. Take these three elements and put them into action in an ever-evolving idea, and you've got a formula for success. For example, Richard Branson started selling records out of the trunk of his car. When the "business" started to grow, he didn't just buy a bigger car with a bigger trunk to hold yet more of his wares. He let the idea *evolve*. And voilà... Virgin Records!

And don't be fooled into thinking that freaks and geeks are anomalies. Hardly. Witness the international phenomenon known as the "Geek Squad," a company built upon offering consumer-based computer (and now home theater) repair and troubleshooting. The employees dress like characters out of *Revenge of the Nerds* but drive cool VW Beetles and sport an "I don't care what you think" hipness.

Look at the Verizon "Can you hear me now?" guy in the commercials. He went from one geeky guy wandering around to the head of a huge network that is loved by its users.

It's cool to be different when you know you bring something unique to the table. People are starting to get that. Witness, for instance, t-shirts that say, "I love nerds" or simply "Nerd." A pop culture fad? I think not. There is a perceptible shift toward recognizing the value in drawing outside the lines. Why, there's even a blog site devoted to geekdom, and each of the bloggers there are bringing huge advances to their businesses. http://www.evancarmichael.com/Tools/Top-50-Entrepreneur-Geek-Blogs-2008.htm

Stop and think about it. What kind of ideas do you have percolating beneath the surface? Is there someone on your team who is just begging to be set free to churn out innovative ideas? Maybe it scares you a bit that they run counter to cultural conventionalism or to the "norms" within your industry or organization. Hey, that's a good thing! No one believed that Steve Jobs could create a single chip that would hold as much memory as it did, either. Over 20 years later, he has helped revolutionize the way we process and communicate information electronically. And, oh yeah, there are those little inventions: iPod, iPhone, and iTunes.

The meek might once have inherited the earth, but the geeks now drive its evolution, and ultimately, this is the unconventional person you want in your organization. This non-linear, no-naysaying energy and momentum defines and builds success!

QUOTE THE NAYSAYER

"There is no reason anyone would want a computer in their home."

**Ken Olson, President, Founder & Chairman,
Digital Equipment Corporation, 1977**

CHAPTER 8: Are You a Naysayer?

> "Aerodynamically, the bumble bee shouldn't be able to fly, but the bumble bee doesn't know it, so it goes on flying anyway."
>
> **MARY KAY ASH**

As you can imagine, there are telltale signs of the chronic naysaying disorder. Unmistakable and downright insidious, these things can derail you before you ever get started. Luckily, with early detection, you can beat the problem before it beats you!

Take the following quiz and answer honestly. You know that old expression, "You're only hurting yourself by acting that way"? Well, it doesn't apply here. If you're going around expounding negative, limiting beliefs, you are indeed hurting yourself, but you're also infecting everything and everyone around you! Stop that!

Answer the questions using the following point scale:

1-Never

2-Sometimes

3-Almost always

4-You mean there's another way of doing it?

1. When asked to devise a new, exciting marketing plan, do you default to dressing up old tried-and-true plans?
2. Are you just dying to break out a multi-media presentation (the likes of which no one has ever seen!) but find yourself irresistibly drawn back to the dry erase board?
3. Do you suspect that those 70–80 percent repeat customers would spread the word about your services if you just had the guts to ask them to invite their friends to your next big event…but then you talk yourself out of asking because the other voice tells you, "It won't work"?
4. Do you think of webinars and podcasts as "too high tech" for most people—a waste of your time and theirs?
5. Do you consider your database an efficient list of contacts rather than a collection of gems of exponential possibility?
6. When you see the opportunity to upsell, do you try to think for the customer and decide not to "bother" them with your opinion?
7. Do you think of creating a referral program as a needless expense?
8. Do you consider blogging to create a buzz to be something only for young MySpacers and lonely lovelorns who don't fit in with your "culture"?
9. If invited to participate in a media launch as part of a huge industry promotion, would you relegate yourself to hanging out by the buffet and chatting with the same people you've had lunch with 7,364 times?
10. During a brainstorming session with your team, do you look for the flaw in each idea before examining its potential?

LET'S TAKE A LOOK AT YOUR SCORES:

- 35-40—You're not only still thinking inside the box that you were told to drop kick, your whole head is stuck inside of it! Pry yourself out and open your eyes to the brilliant light of possibilities!
- 30-35—You're slowly suffocating, but you're not beyond hope! You at least peer outside of the box once in a while.
- 25-30—You say "nay" much more than you should, but you are at least aware of the possibilities out there!
- 20-25—You've probably got some very creative thinking friends who are starting to influence you. Let them!
- 15-20—You're teetering on the fence but starting to feel more comfortable with creative thinking.
- 10-15—You seldom see limits to what you and others can accomplish.
- A perfect 10! The sky's the limit. Look for your name on future most-influential-and-successful-people-in-the-world lists!

Regardless of your score, you're reading this book because you are (or want to be) an agent for change. You want to improve yourself as a whole...and not just your professional life. Thinking creatively is the best way to do that. If you ever doubt it, just re-read the introductory section and revisit the brilliant people who have affected your life by never saying NAY!

QUOTE THE NAYSAYER

"We don't like their sound, and guitar music is on the way out."

Decca Recording Company, on rejecting The Beatles, 1962

SUMMARY:

> "Success usually comes to those who are too busy to be looking for it."
>
> **HENRY DAVID THOREAU**

The votes are in. Hands down, the positive, creative thinkers win! Not only have they been the movers and shakers of the past, but they continue to usher in the innovations that keep our world, and probably your organization, turning in increasingly interesting and efficient ways. Even cleverly disguised as buttoned-up "business people," these men and women bring a dynamic energy to any project or organization by default. The power in creative thinking is that it feeds off itself, creating and encouraging more creative thinking. And that kind of energy is what lays the groundwork for the future in every passing second.

> *"The last few decades have belonged to a certain kind of person with a certain kind of mind—computer programmers who could crank code, lawyers who could craft contracts, MBAs who could crunch numbers. But the keys to the kingdom are changing hands. The future belongs to a very different kind of person with a very different kind of mind—creators and empathizers, pattern recognizers and meaning makers. These people—artists, inventors, designers, storytellers, caregivers, consolers, big picture thinkers—will now reap society's richest rewards and share its greatest joys."*
>
> - Dan Pink, *A Whole New Mind*

Pink is not saying here that MBAs, lawyers, and programmers are on the fast track to extinction. What he is saying is that to survive, such people will have to adopt big picture, creative thinking. So, that idea in your head, that marketing plan, that next campaign, that inkling you have about creating better and more authentic relationships with your customers give it a voice, give it a paradigm in which to grow, and then give it wings to touch and shape the lives it will. Welcome to the world of creative thinking. What's on your mind?

QUOTE THE NAYSAYER

"The concept is interesting and well-formed, but in order to earn better than a 'C,' the idea must be feasible."

A Yale University management professor, responding to Fred Smith's paper proposing reliable overnight delivery service.

Smith later founded Federal Express Corporation.

RESOURCES

> "You can't build a reputation on what you are going to do."
>
> **HENRY FORD**

So, are you ready to rethink the way you interact with your colleagues, the way you approach your projects, the way you do business? If you see yourself reflected in these pages, then putting a positive spin on your style will mean one thing for certain: your professional life will snag a big boost from a creative thinking overhaul.

Don't be fooled, though; even with the best intentions, change is not easy. You won't wake up tomorrow ready to discard a lifetime's worth of naysaying. Expect to stumble; you might even fall. But having a list of resources at your fingertips for easy referral will help you to create new habits. Peruse the following websites on a regular basis for help with creating new thoughts and actions.

- **www.creativityincubator.com** This site offers specific tools to kick-start your creativity. "It's for managers and executives, decision-makers and influencers — people who are actively seeking new and better ways of doing things in their organization."
- **www.creativity-portal.com** Creativity Portal is exactly what the name says: an entry to a world of innovation — and humor. Discover the important role of fun, humor, and playtime in the creative process.
- **www.webdistortion.com** This web design company is based in Ireland and "thinks a bit different". Their blog page is a perfect reflection of that fact, and a fantastic resource for topics like this one: "Creative Business Thinking: Five ways to new products or services".

- **www.evancarmichael.com** Talk about a wealth of resources! This site offers clickable links for everything from Advertising to Going Green to Technology. You can even find personal, engaging success stories from the likes of Calvin Klein. And their blog page is extremely diverse, even branching off into a page that celebrates the glory of geekdom: http://www.evancarmichael.com/Tools/Top-50-Entrepreneur-Geek-Blogs-2008.htm
- **www.debonogroup.com** "We believe thinking is the ultimate human resource" is one of their mottos. This is the site for a consulting company, but you'll find a great explanation of the tools they use, as well, that can inspire your own creative thinking.
- **http://learninglaboratory.blogspot.com/2005/11/creative-thinking-in-business-and.html** This is a blog written by an educational consultant. She says, "Creativity is often thought of as a singular quality -- an attractive intangible, a soft skill, a gauzy perspective. At worst, it's thought to preclude common sense or practical application. In fact, innovative thinking is not nearly so obscure." She also lists skill sets that you certainly have at your disposal. Read on at the site!

These sites will get you started, linking up with the endless resources that are out there, just waiting to support you in your new commitment to creative thinking. Any web search for "creative thinking in business" will bring up more sites than you'll know what to do with. And just what, in fact, will you do with so much creativity just waiting to be set free? You will succeed beyond your wildest dreams…and do it all with more joy than you have ever imagined!

About the Author

A dedicated marketing professional, Michelle Kabele has been helping technology companies develop award-winning channel partner programs and marketing strategies for over 10 years. Her innovative channel marketing concepts have been adopted and implemented by many leading technology companies, including Zebra Technologies, 3Com Corporation, and U.S. Robotics.

Moreover, Michelle has worked extensively with VARs throughout North America and thoroughly understands the realities and practicalities they face in planning and executing effective promotional, marketing, and sales campaigns.

Michelle has an MBA from the J.L. Kellogg Graduate School of Management (Evanston, IL) and an undergraduate degree from Northwestern University (Evanston, IL). For more great ways to build your business, check out all of Michelle Kabele's books:

Great Marketing Is Free!

All the Web's A Stage

50 Smart, Easy and Effective Ideas to Boost Your Business Today

Visit www.ideastormpress.com for up-to-the-minute news, advice, ideas, and just cool stuff.

www.ingramcontent.com/pod-product-compliance
Lightning Source LLC
LaVergne TN
LVHW010549100826
845148LV00013B/2674

* 9 7 8 0 9 8 2 0 6 8 6 3 2 *